A gift for:

_____

From:

_____

How to Use Your Interactive Story Buddy™:

1. Activate your Story Buddy™ by pressing the "On / Off" button on the ear.
2. Read the story aloud in a quiet place. Speak in a clear voice when you see the highlighted phrases.
3. Listen to your Story Buddy™ respond with several different phrases throughout the book.

Clarity and speed of reading affect the way Nugget™ responds. He may not always respond to young children.

Watch for even more Interactive Storybooks & Story Buddy™ characters. For more information, visit us on the Web at Hallmark.com/StoryBuddy.

Copyright © 2012 Hallmark Licensing, LLC

Published by Hallmark Gift Books,
a division of Hallmark Cards, Inc.,
Kansas City, MO 64141
Visit us on the Web at Hallmark.com.

Editor: Chelsea Fogleman
Art Director: Kevin Swanson
Designer: Brian Pilachowski
Production Designer: Bryan Ring

ISBN: 978-1-59530-441-4
SKU: PSB4117

Printed and bound in China
MAR12

Hallmark's **I Reply Technology** brings your Story Buddy™ to life! When you read the key phrases out loud, your Story Buddy™ gives a variety of responses, so each time you read feels as magical as the first.

BOOK 1

Nugget's
First Day of School

BY **Molly Wigand** ILLUSTRATED BY **Sandy Koeser**

Hallmark
GIFT BOOKS

One morning, Nugget heard the leash and
car keys jingle. His tail wagged so fast, he couldn't
stand still. He just knew today would be a great day.
They were getting in the car. And there was
nothing better than a ride in the car!

Nugget pressed his nose against the window and watched as they drove past all kinds of places: the dog food store, the dog doctor, and the burger place.

When they stopped, Nugget jumped out of the car and sniffed the ground. It smelled like dogs. Lots of dogs.

Nugget's kids gave him big good-bye hugs. "Be a good boy," they said. "We'll see you really soon!" Nugget was confused. His kids were leaving?

Nugget loved his family more than anyone could imagine.

Inside the strange new place, Nugget saw big dogs and small dogs. Curly dogs and spotted dogs. Old dogs and tiny puppies. It looked like they were having lots of fun.

All these dogs seemed to know each other. But Nugget didn't know anyone.

Soon other dogs ran over to see the new pup.

A big brown dog bent down to introduce himself. "Hey, buddy! My name is Hugo. Welcome to Doggy School!"

A curly poodle announced, "My name is Victoria. It's splendid that you're here!"

Nugget frowned. "Well, I don't think it's so great," he said. "I miss my family."

Nugget felt kind of sad.

A long, stretchy dog ran to Nugget's side.

"I'm Pickle!" he said, panting and wagging his tail.

"Want to chase me? Or I can chase you! Or we can chase the other pups!"

"No thanks," said Nugget. "I'm going to wait by the door for my family."

Nugget was getting a little lonely. He wanted to go home more than anything.

Then, all of a sudden, Nugget heard some strange sounds. With a thump, a plastic disc landed next to his head.

This made Nugget a little curious.

"Hey, buddy!" Hugo barked at Nugget. "Want to play?"

Nugget's tail wagged one little wag. He did love flying discs.

Nugget took the disc to the teacher so she could toss it.

Hugo cheered. "Go long, buddy!"

Pickle giggled. "Hey! It's my job to go LONG! Get it? Long?"

All the dogs laughed. Even Nugget.

The teacher threw the disc across the room. Nugget ran as fast as he could and jumped . . . and he caught the flying disc!

The other dogs cried, "Hooray!" **And to his own surprise, Nugget was super-duper happy.**

"That was fun!" said Nugget. "But now I'm going to wait for my family again."

Victoria was primping her curls. "All right," she said. "You'll miss treat time, though." She pranced over to a line of shiny dog dishes.

"Treat time?" asked Nugget.

He slowly made his way to Victoria's side and peered down into a food bowl.

The idea of a treat made Nugget a little curious.

Newt

Buffy

Hugo was first to take a bite. "Over the lips and through the gums! Look out, tummy! Here it comes!" He swallowed the treat while drool flew everywhere.

Laughing, Victoria clucked her tongue. "Hugo, that's gross!" She dabbed her face clean with the back of a paw.

This treat was different from Nugget's bone-shaped treats at home.

"Try it!" said Pickle, smacking his mouth. "It's scrumptious!"

Nugget took a tiny taste. Then his tail wagged. "What IS this?"

"Bacon!" the other dogs sang.

Nugget thought it was the tastiest food in the world!

After a while, Nugget said, "I'm getting sleepy!" He plopped on the ground.

"Me, too," yawned Hugo. He snuggled next to Nugget. Victoria neatly lowered herself beside Hugo. Pickle wiggled in and cuddled up, too.

With a happy sigh, Nugget settled down for a nice doggy nap.

Nugget was in the middle of a great dream about bacon, flying discs, and new dog friends.

Then someone patted his back. Nugget opened one sleepy eye. His kids were here to pick him up! His tail wagged like crazy.

Nugget loved his family more than anyone could imagine.

But Nugget liked his new friends, too!

He woke up Hugo. "I have to leave," he whimpered.

"That's okay," Hugo replied. "You'll come back again."

"We're going home soon, too," Victoria added.

"See you next time!" said Pickle.

On the way home, his kids asked, "Did you like
school, Nugget?"

"Ruff! Ruff!" Nugget barked. He was so happy
to be with family again. But he was also excited about
tomorrow—because then he might get to go to school
again. And Nugget absolutely loved going to school!

Did you have fun going to school with Nugget?

We would love to hear from you.

Please send your comments to:

Hallmark Book Feedback

P.O. Box 419034

Mail Drop 215

Kansas City, MO 64141

Or e-mail us at:

booknotes@hallmark.com